No Room for Sarah

Story and Pictures by Ann Greenleaf

Dodd, Mead & Company • New York

Library of Congress Cataloging in Publication Data

Greenleaf, Ann, 1946-
No room for Sarah.

Summary. Because of the size of Sarah's bed, her
father says her stuffed animals have to go — a decision
which effects the animals and family so adversely that
another solution must be found.
[1. Bedtime — Fiction.   2. Toys — Fiction]   I. Title.
PZ7.G846No   1983   [E]   83-9044
ISBN 0-396-08213-0

For Aaron

"Come kiss me good night," Sarah shouted to her parents from the top of the stairs.

"Did you brush your teeth?" called her mother.

"All except one," Sarah yelled, "but it didn't look dirty."

"All right dear. We'll be right there."

But Sarah was nowhere in sight.

"Tuck me in!" came a voice from the bed.

"Who's that?" said Sarah's father. "Brown Dog? Bamboo Bear? Hoppin' Bunno?"

"It's me. Sarah! Tuck me in."

"I would if I could find you," he said.

"I think I see a foot," said Sarah's mother, "and a blonde pigtail over there."

"Sarah, this can't be comfortable," her father said. "There's no room for you. I am sorry, but some of these animals will have to go."

"But I always sleep with *all* my animals. You know that."

"You didn't always *have* all these animals. Narrow it down to two for tonight or you'll never get to sleep."

"But the others will be jealous."

"No buts," said her father, "and no more nonsense."

It won't work, Sarah said to herself as her parents left the room.

Sarah had just fallen asleep when something made her sit up with a start. Brown Dog was standing on her stomach.

"What's the big idea?" he snarled. "Picking Bubble Beak and Hose Nose when you could have picked me!"

"Yeah, or me," Teddy whined. He pulled Brown Dog out of bed and crawled in himself.

No sooner had Teddy settled in than Squawkin' Hawk shoved him to the floor. In no time at all a full-scale fight broke out.

It was, of course, impossible to sleep with twenty stuffed animals kicking and screaming, so Sarah crawled into bed with her parents.

"No more musical beds at midnight," her father said the next morning at breakfast. "No one in this house got a wink of sleep."

"Thanks to *you*," Sarah said. "My animals were up all night fighting."

"Sarah, if your animals can't get along, they'll all have to sleep on the floor tonight and that's that."

"They're not going to like it," Sarah warned.

"I can live with a stuffed donkey being mad at me," her father said, "but I cannot do without my sleep."

That night Sarah was tucked into bed without a single animal.

"I think this will work fine," her mother said.

I don't, Sarah said to herself.

And Sarah was right. From the minute her head hit the pillow, it was:

"Sarah, sniffle, sniffle, you don't love us anymore," and,

"Boohoo, boohoo, life is so hard and so is this floor," and,

"Oh, woe, woe, woe is me!"

It was, of course, impossible to sleep with twenty stuffed animals weeping and wailing, so Sarah crawled into bed with her parents.

"They won't stop bawling till they're back in my bed," she explained.

"Oh, dear," said Sarah's mother. "Perhaps we'd better go cheer them up."

"No one's going anywhere," said Sarah's father. "They'll pipe down if we just ignore them. Take my word for it."

The next morning Sarah's father could barely lift his head to drink his coffee.

"Young lady," he said, "I'm at my wit's end. You turned and squirmed till 5:00 A.M. If you can't work something out with your animals, they'll just have to go. And that's final."

Sarah looked to her mother for help, but her mother was almost asleep.

Two adults against one little child, Sarah thought. It's not fair. "Mom, are you going to have any more kids?"

"No, dear. I'm too tired. But maybe if I got some sleep."

"Okay, okay. I'll give them away." For a while, Sarah added to herself.

Katie next door and Laura down the street agreed to take ten animals apiece until things blew over at Sarah's.

That night the house was very quiet. Sarah had decided she would never speak to her parents again. All through dinner they tried to get her to talk to them. But Sarah just wrote "Good Night" on a paper airplane, sailed it into the living room, slammed her bedroom door, and went to bed.

Three minutes before midnight she heard a tapping at her window.

"Hey, Sarah. Let me in! I've got a friend here I want you to meet."

What else could she do? She let Donkey and his friend in.

Two seconds later Monkey was yelling, "Hey, Sarah, have a heart. Me and my buddies are freezing out here."

It was, of course, impossible to sleep with twenty stuffed animals and their guests knocking at her window, so Sarah propped it open and snuggled into bed with her parents.

Sarah's father opened one eye. "Go back to bed," he said.

"Can't," she said. "They're all home again and they've brought twenty friends."

"They're your animals, Sarah. Go make them behave."

"*You* make them behave. *You* made them leave."

"Dear," said Sarah's mother, "I think your father would rather have a word with them in the morning. Now good night, everyone. And Sarah, could you please remove your foot from my head?"

"Sarah," her mother said at breakfast, "this nighttime commotion cannot go on. What are we going to do?"

"Let's divide the animals between our two beds," Sarah suggested. "What do you like? Bunnies? Birds? Bears?"

Her mother was too tired to argue. "How about the elephant?" she said weakly.

"She's too shy," Sarah said. "You can have the giraffe."

"A giraffe?! In *my bed*? Ellen, have you lost your senses?" her father yelled at her mother. He rarely yelled, but of course he hadn't slept for three nights.

Sarah's mother stood up. "Sarah and I will be sorting animals. When you feel you can talk without raising your voice, we would be happy to hear if you have any better ideas. I want to get some sleep tonight."

Sarah's father knocked on the door and poked his head into the room.

"I've come up to apologize," he said, "and to tell you I've hit upon a solution to our animal problem. It's so simple I don't know why we didn't think of it before. Sarah just needs a bigger bed!"

"It will have to be very big," Sarah pointed out. "I had close to forty animals last night."

"It will be as big as you need."

They set to work immediately. It took all day, but when they were done…

Sarah had a bed that filled the room. It could sleep one child, twenty animals, and any number of unexpected guests.

That night they were feeling very pleased with themselves and were all looking forward to a good long sleep.

"Sarah," her mother called after dinner. "Are you ready for bed?"

"Most of me is," Sarah yelled from her room, "but the big toe on my right foot is not the least bit tired."

"Well, read it a story, dear," her mother suggested, "and we'll be up shortly to tuck you in."

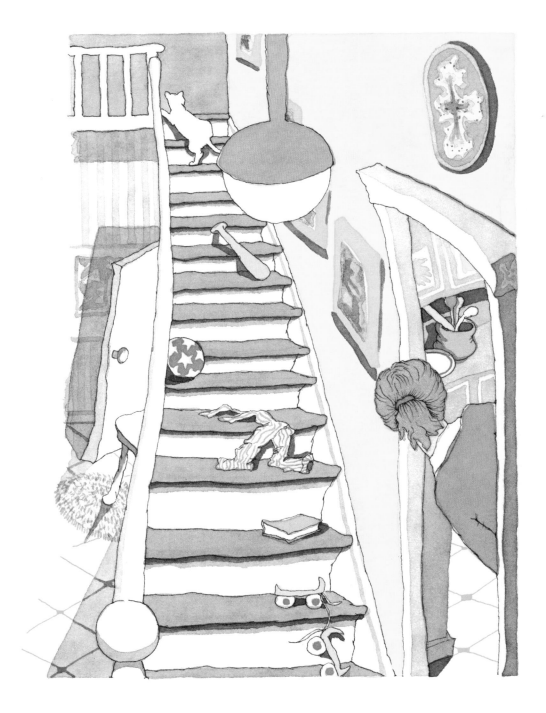

Sarah's parents opened the door to her room and beamed. The big bed had worked. Sarah and her animals were already snoring. There was plenty of room for everyone.

"It just goes to show you what can be done if we all work together to solve a problem," Sarah's mother said.

"Yes, indeed," said Sarah's father. "Now we'll get some sleep."

And they all did.